Dear Parents:

Congratulations! Your child is taking the first steps on an exciting journey. The destination? Independent reading!

STEP INTO READING® will help your child get there. The program offers five steps to reading success. Each step includes fun stories and colorful art or photographs. In addition to original fiction and books with favorite characters, there are Step into Reading Non-Fiction Readers, Phonics Readers and Boxed Sets, Sticker Readers, and Comic Readers—a complete literacy program with something to interest every child.

Learning to Read, Step by Step!

Ready to Read   Preschool–Kindergarten
• big type and easy words • rhyme and rhythm • picture clues
For children who know the alphabet and are eager to begin reading.

Reading with Help   Preschool–Grade 1
• basic vocabulary • short sentences • simple stories
For children who recognize familiar words and sound out new words with help.

Reading on Your Own   Grades 1–3
• engaging characters • easy-to-follow plots • popular topics
For children who are ready to read on their own.

Reading Paragraphs   Grades 2–3
• challenging vocabulary • short paragraphs • exciting stories
For newly independent readers who read simple sentences with confidence.

Ready for Chapters   Grades 2–4
• chapters • longer paragraphs • full-color art
For children who want to take the plunge into chapter books but still like colorful pictures.

STEP INTO READING® is designed to give every child a successful reading experience. The grade levels are only guides; children will progress through the steps at their own speed, developing confidence in their reading.

Remember, a lifetime love of reading starts with a single step!

For Graham
—N.E.

Special thanks to Kelsey Howard,
Sherin Kwan, and Alex Wiltshire

All rights reserved. Published in the United States by Random House Children's Books, a division of Penguin Random House LLC, 1745 Broadway, New York, NY 10019, and in Canada by Penguin Random House Canada Limited, Toronto.

Step into Reading, Random House, and the Random House colophon are registered trademarks of Penguin Random House LLC.

Visit us on the Web!
StepIntoReading.com
rhcbooks.com
minecraft.net
Educators and librarians, for a variety of teaching tools, visit us at RHTeachersLibrarians.com

ISBN 978-0-593-37267-8 (trade) — ISBN 978-0-593-37268-5 (lib. bdg.) —
ISBN 978-0-593-37269-2 (ebook)

Printed in the United States of America
10 9 8 7 6 5 4 3

MINECRAFT

SURVIVAL MODE!

by Nick Eliopulos

illustrated by Alan Batson

Random House 🏠 New York

Emmy blinked and looked around.

It was a bright new morning

in the Minecraft Overworld.

Bees were buzzing.

Cows were grazing.

Chickens were pecking.

Her best friend, Birch,
was already there,
playing in the sunflowers
with his pet wolf, Byte.

But Emmy knew that
when the sun went down,
monsters would return.
"Let's get serious,"
she said. "We don't have
any time to waste."
"What's your plan?" asked Birch.
Emmy *always* had a plan.

"Today, we will climb
to the very top
of Mount Farview,"
said Emmy, "and see
what we can see!"
Birch gasped. Mount Farview
was the tallest mountain around.

Emmy and Birch both knew
they would need supplies
to travel so far.
Byte barked loudly.
He pointed his nose
at an oak tree.

"Good idea, Byte," said Emmy.

"We should get wood right away."

"I'll do it!" said Birch.

He punched the tree.

The tree broke apart

into blocks of wood.

When they had enough logs,
Emmy made oak planks.

She used the planks
to create a crafting table.

"Now we can make tools," Emmy said.
"We'll craft a shovel, a pickaxe,
and a sword—maybe an axe."
"Make an extra pickaxe
for me!" said Birch.

Now that they had wooden tools,
Emmy, Birch, and Byte
started walking
toward the mountain.

They saw a spider lurking
beneath a tree.
Birch was ready for it,
but the spider would not attack
in daylight. It only watched
them with its beady red eyes.

Finally, they came
to the end of the plain.
They now stood at the foot
of Mount Farview.
The mountain was tall.
Birch could not see the top.
Byte howled—*AWOOOO!*

"We should gather
more supplies," said Emmy.
She used her axe
to knock apples
out of an oak tree.
Birch used his pickaxe
to gather cobblestone.

Without warning,

Birch's pickaxe broke!

The wooden tool shattered

against the hard stone mountain.

"Don't be sad, Birch," said Emmy.

"I can use my crafting table

to make a new pickaxe for you."

Now Birch had a pickaxe
made of stone.
It was stronger
than his wooden one.

"Thanks, Emmy!"
said Birch, and he smiled.

Together, the friends climbed
the mountain until the sun
was low in the sky.
"Soon it will be night,"
said Emmy. "We should stop
and build a shelter—
before the monsters come."

They worked as a team.
While Birch mined
more cobblestones,
Emmy began stacking blocks
to make the walls of a house.
Byte was no help. He just
chased a chicken.

Suddenly, an arrow whizzed

through the air.

It landed by Emmy's foot—*THUNK!*

It was too late

to finish the house!

"It's a skeleton!"
cried Birch.
He raised his pickaxe.
He was not going to let
a hostile mob shoot arrows
at his friend!

Birch charged at the skeleton, and Byte dashed after him! Emmy pulled out her sword.

The skeleton reached
for another arrow,
but Byte bit him on the leg!
The skeleton wobbled
as it tried to aim.

Birch hit it with a swing
of his pickaxe!
And Emmy delivered
the final blow
to the mob.

"Good job!" said Emmy.
"But now there will be
more monsters.
And we have nowhere
to hide."

"We can take them,"

Birch said.

"Fighting monsters is scary—

and fun!"

The night was long,
and the path
up the mountain
was dangerous.

Emmy, Birch, and Byte
fought all the zombies,
skeletons, and creepers
that spawned in their path.

When the sun rose,
the final zombie
burst into flames!
Now they could finish
their journey.

"We made it," said Emmy.
They stepped onto
the snowy peak
of the mountain.

Emmy and Birch could see a desert,
a swamp, a forest, and an ocean.
The Overworld was a big place,
and their adventures were just beginning.